Original title, *Heks*
Published by Free Musketeers

Drakonia the Witch

Elizabeth Deckers

America Star Books

First printing

All characters in this book are fictitious, and any resemblance to real persons, living or dead, is coincidental.

Portrait: Adrie Deckers

Softcover 9781633827967
PUBLISHED BY AMERICA STAR BOOKS, LLLP
www.americastarbooks.com

Chapter 1

Oh there you are, Drakonia!

The beautiful witch with her bright blue eyes and long blonde hair.

Have you met Drakonia yet?

Then I'm going to tell you a story about her.

Drakonia the witch is very beautiful and sweet.

She likes wearing beautiful dresses like that of a real princess.

But Drakonia is not sweet. In fact, Drakonia is a witch…a very old witch and has done a lot of harm.

Although she's old, she looks radiant and young. People say she can enchant you with her beautiful smile.

Today, Drakonia is creating a new potion, a drink to change children into spiders. She will have more fun with spiders than with children. She laughs loudly and crisply as she says to herself,

"Haha, soon there will be no children with dirty hands, who only make noise and create mess."

She stirs in a big cauldron and sings softly.
"Stirring, stirring, full of good sense. Throw some mosquitoes' feet. This will change every child into a spider."

The dirty mud in the boiler starts to simmer and smoke. The stench is almost unbearable but she doesn't seem to mind. She breathes the vapors deeply and smiles like she smells freshly baked pancakes.

As Drakonia stirs and sings, the mud slowly turns to a greenish brown beverage. It turns to yellow, then purple, and finally to a nice pink color. The smell disappears and Drakonia's kitchen suddenly smells like raspberry candies. The drink starts to foam and turns to lemonade...raspberry lemonade!

Drakonia is pleased as she looks in her cauldron and sings and stirs for awhile.

She taps her foot on the floor and begins to sing a new song.

"Oh what a wonderful smell, oh delicious fragrance,
Lock those awful kids at my door,
Let me enjoy pouring these drinks in small glasses,
Drink, drink children,
Then be a spider, strong and big."

Drakonia momentarily looks in the boiler and smiles with satisfaction. The potion needs to cool down before it can be served in small glasses.

Drakonia hastily leaves her kitchen as she realizes she has plenty more to do.

Chapter 2

First, Drakonia wants the basement to be perfect. All children turned into spiders will be locked in the basement.

Drakonia opens the heavy door with difficulty and it creaks and groans as it slides. Behind the door is a wide stone staircase and it is dark like the middle of the night without stars and moon. Drakonia grabs the lamp hanging on the door and mutters,
"Light in my hands, go burn rapidly,
Give me light, very bright."

The light flashes briefly and a bright blue light appears. The lamp lights the steps of what seems a thousand staircases but Drakonia stepped down merrily.

Down the stairs is another door larger than the first one at the top of the stairs. The door is so big and heavy that Drakonia has to use a spell to open and close it. Drakonia stands at the door, taps the dark wood and says,

"Spider, spider, spider, let me in."

The door opens slowly. Behind it is a cold, dark, and large underground cave. The cave seems to be illuminated with eight small lights. But when Drakonia holds her lamp up, the eight small lights are actually the eyes of four spiders hanging in thick cobwebs on the rough stone walls.

Drakonia focuses her light on the spider web at the far corner of the cave. The spider hanging in the thick web is wearing a little crown on her head. The witch looks at the spider and puts a beautiful smile on her face. She starts talking to the spider in her false and crispy voice.

"Hello, spinning Princess Esmeralda! Don't you think my dress is nicer than yours?
I have good news for you, Princess. From now on, you will have lots of friends."

Big tears start to slip from the eyes of Princess Esmeralda, the spider wearing a crown. She's the first child transformed by Drakonia into a spider.

Princess Esmeralda is crying not because she has been changed into a spider. She's crying because Drakonia is going to turn more children into spiders and she doesn't want other children to be enchanted.

Chapter 3

The old shack where Drakonia lives is well hidden in the forest. In the middle of a large garden behind the forest, the king and queen of the country live in a magnificent palace. The palace has towers with white walls and golden crowns, and shiny red tiles on the roofs.

The king and queen are Princess Esmeralda's parents. Despite the beauty of the palace and gardens, the king and queen are sad. The queen has been crying while the king grieved at his beard all day because Princess Esmeralda has not yet been found.

It seems just a few days ago when Princess Esmeralda was playing with her dog Charlie and suddenly she disappeared. Charlie was shaking with fear as he ran inside. The queen immediately ran outside looking for the princess but she was nowhere to be seen.

Everyone in the castle was called to look for Princess Esmeralda. Everyone looked in the garden, at the pond, at the tea house, in the labyrinth, even in the stables with the horses. Every room in the palace was searched, from cases to caskets, from under every bed to old attics in the towers. However, the princess remained missing.

The brave knights on horses searched all the major places in the country and, along the way; they asked everyone to look for the princess as well. Everyone in the country has been looking for Princess Esmeralda.

The king and queen become sadder every day and can't sleep at night as the princess has not yet been found. Every day, Charlie walks around the palace sniffing in search of his dear master. After searching to no avail, he lies in his basket and grieves.

Where can the sweet princess be?

Chapter 4

Meanwhile, Drakonia looks around the cold dark basement and makes sure the spiders can't escape. After looking around, she turns to the spider with the crown. "Do not cry my dear Princess Esmeralda. Soon, there will be lots of spiders to play with."

She turns around and says the spell to close the heavy door again, "Close, close door, leaves no spider out." The heavy door slides shut and Drakonia slowly climbs the long stairs to the top and goes to her room.

The wall of Drakonia's room is covered with mirrors. She stops at the mirror and happily looks at her reflection. She makes a few faces at herself and admires her beautiful face. She turns to her closet and picks up the most beautiful dress.

The dress is from Princess Esmeralda and Drakonia has stolen it from her. It is made from expensive pink silk, printed with little bunnies and decorated with lots of gems.

Drakonia pulls the pretty dress and goes back to the mirror to admire it. She starts brushing the dress like it's a shiny long hair.

Skipping and singing, Drakonia goes back to the kitchen and sits down on the wooden table where an old and thick book lies. The book is not just an ordinary book, it's the witch's big bad spells book.

Drakonia pulls the book closer to her and starts turning pages. She continues turning the pages until she finds the right spell. She reads the spell a couple of times until she memorizes it in her head.

She walks to the door, opens it, and looks around. In the doorway, the trees and shrubs grow closer to her old hovel. From the hovel, she looks towards the village and calls,

"Listen, forest and heath, create a path from the village to me. Hang lots of candies and cakes in the trees, and make sure the children come to me."

Then, a path appears among the trees and plants towards the village. The path runs from the old shack to the school in the village and all the way to gate of the school.

The trees and bushes along the path are filled with cookies and candies. Some branches are so heavy that they bend so that cookies and candies are on the path. Not only does the path look very enticing, it also smells delicious, like newly baked cookies.

Drakonia closes her door and walks into her cauldron of magic potion. The drink has become cold and she starts pouring the drink to the small glasses.

"So...let the spiders, uhh, kids come," mutters the witch.

Chapter 5

In the village, the school is just starting and all children are on the playground... laughing, talking, making playmates with each other. It's like any ordinary day in the school.

Once the kids in the schoolyard are out, they smell the delicious freshly baked cookies. Then they see the irresistible candy-filled trees and bushes. All children start to get excited and walk the path while putting candies in their mouths.

They are too busy eating goodies that they haven't paid attention to where they are going. They haven't noticed that they are going the wrong direction, away from the village and deeper into the forest.

At the back of the group of children is a quiet but very smart guy. His name is Tristan and he's the smartest in his class. He just looks at the goodies but is not interested in eating them. Tristan's father has died recently and he now lives in the village with his mother, and twin siblings Anton and Benthe.

Tristan adores his twin siblings. Tristan's mother doesn't have much money and most often, she can't buy Tristan and his siblings nice things.

Looking at the candies, Tristan reaches for his backpack. Instead of helping his self into the goodies, he thinks of his mother and little siblings.

He puts a piece of candy in his mouth and puts sweets and biscuits in his backpack. Tristan imagines the look on his family's faces when he surprises them with treats. Tristan takes a few big chocolates to his lunchbox as he remembers his mother.

Then, Tristan sees the largest chocolate bar he has ever seen. He immediately thinks of his sister who loves chocolate so much. "Chocowa" as Benthe calls it. Laughing, he puts the chocolate bar in his backpack.

He also sees thick licorice hanging on the tree branches and he thinks of his brother

Anton. He quickly grabs a lot of licorice into his backpack as he imagines his brother's delighted face.

Tristan decides he has collected enough candies and closes his backpack. He notices he's behind the group and he comes running to catch them. He sees the first group of children go inside the old shack. With his heavy backpack, Tristan struggles to run fast.

When he almost catches up with the group, he notices that his shoelace has gone loose and quickly does his shoelace firmly. As he stands up again, the last child goes inside the house as the door closes.

Tristan walks around the cottage with old, dilapidated, and dirty windows. He looks through the window pane and sees a beautiful woman in a pretty dress handing small glasses of lemonade to the children. Thirsty from the sweets they have eaten, they drink and empty their glasses quickly.

Tristan continues to look around the house and just as he would knock on the door, he jumps in shock. Staggering, he runs back away from the house and into the village.

Tristan rubs his eyes in disbelief; he could not believe what he has seen. He must have been dreaming but it's impossible to be dreaming in the middle of the day.

Slowly, he sneaks back to the old house and carefully looks again through the window. All children from his school are gone and the floor of the old shack is full of walking spiders. The woman in the cottage has turned the children into spiders with the lemonade!

Tristan sits down to think. What should he do? Should he get help? But who will believe him? Tristan hardly believes himself for what he has seen...and what is that woman going to do with the children she has turned into spiders?

Tristan is convinced that the woman is no good. The beautiful woman must be a witch, an evil witch who turns children into spiders. But what will she do with the spiders? Maybe she's going to use the spiders to make more potions?

'Go, I must do something and think fast.' Tristan thinks to his self. He must solve this on his own.

He looks again through the dirty window and the witch is back in the kitchen. He ducks down under the window and thinks of a plan. But no matter how smart he is, nothing comes to his mind. When he looks again through the window, he looks straight into a pair of big blue eyes...the eyes of the witch!

The door of the old house flies open and there she is, the witch with a radiant smile on her pretty face. The sun's rays reflect off her beautiful dress as she stands outside the house looking like an angel than a witch. In her hand, she holds a glass of lemonade.

"Come on kid," she said sweetly. "I have a nice glass of lemonade."

Tristan knows better but what should he do? He doesn't have a choice and slowly, he puts the glass on his lips. He opens his mouth to take a sip and then suddenly, Tristan throws the drink on the witch's face!

The radiant smile of the witch disappeared. Her big blue eyes are squeezed into narrow stripes. Her rosy red lips are now colorless and pressed together, her whole face distorted with rage.

Tristan heard Drakonia blazing on angry tone, "You little brat! Do you think you are so smart that you can escape?"

The witch is fierce!

Chapter 6

The furious witch starts screaming and tries to address the kid. Tristan tries to run away but the witch grabs his coat and gets hold of him by the collar. Tristan tries to yank but the witch is too strong. She drags him inside the house and slams the door shut.

Tristan stumbles and mows his arm but Drakonia doesn't let go of him and says in a scratchy voice, "You, too, can't escape. You will also become a spider!"

Tristan watches around anxiously as the witch holds him tightly. He has no chance to escape. Then suddenly, a strange noise erupts...

PLOPPPP!

And Tristan is on the ground.

Tristan looks up in confusion and crawls away from the witch. Drakonia grabs her face and shrieks. She staggers to a mirror and sees her beautiful face turned into a hairy spider's web. Drakonia looks like a spider's web with bulging eyes. Her long blonde hair is now gone, her head is covered with dark spines.

Drakonia shrieks and turns around to Tristan. She wants to enchant the kid with a spell but as she points to Tristan, she stops. She lost all her spells which makes her even more furious.

Tristan stands up and looks toward the cauldron of magic potion. The witch runs to the cauldron but Tristan reaches it first. He picks up the cauldron and holds it tightly. He threatens to throw the potion at the witch so Drakonia backs off.

Tristan is now a little less afraid of the witch as long as he has the cauldron of magic potion. Nothing can happen to him as he holds on to the magic potion, at least that's what he hopes for.

Drakonia is trying to get closer and Tristan makes a sweeping motion with the cauldron and so Drakonia steps back again.

Suddenly, Tristan thinks of an idea to help the children. He looks at Drakonia and says, "You're a terrible witch! I can turn you into a spider but I want you to make a new drink, a drink to turn my school friends back from spiders. If you won't, I'll change you to a spider!"

"Szzzkannn niieeet..." The sound that comes out of the spider's web is impossible to understand. Tristan acts like he's going to throw the potion and Drakonia steps back again.

"Make a potion that will work NOW!" Tristan says sternly.

Still, the witch does nothing. Suddenly, the witch steps forward and hold the bottom of the cauldron. Tristan is not prepared for this and the cauldron wobbles in his hands. As the cauldron continues to wobble, a little potion pours out of the cauldron and spills on the dress of Drakonia. When she notices the spilled drink on her dress, she lets go of the cauldron. The witch feels the cold drink on her legs.

"Nnnneeeeehhhhzzz," Tristan hears her say.

Then again...

PLOP! PLOP!

Drakonia begins to falter and looks startled at her legs. But instead of her legs, there are now two long spider legs under her dress. In order not to fall, she grabs on the table and anxiously looks at Tristan.

Tristan holds the cauldron of potion firmly and walks to the witch. He keeps the cauldron before her, attempting to throw more potion on the witch.

Drakonia looks back to the cauldron terrifyingly and says, "Zzzoookkkeee, nietttzzzz meezzz zzzgooiennn, zzik zzzgaa zzzdrank makezzzz."

Chapter 7

The witch struggles to sit on a chair and grabs the old spells book. Tristan is watching closely as the witch begins to turn the pages of the book. Drakonia is looking for the recipe of the potion to change back the children again.

When she finds the right page, Drakonia staggers with her spider legs to the cabinet filled with pots, cups, and bottles. Tristan sees jars with spawn, bird legs, and pots with animal eyes, powders, and liquids. The ceiling is filled with large forest leaves, herbs, and dried flowers. Drakonia grabs the ingredients she needs and put everything on the table.

The witch grabs the largest pan hanging on the walls with other copper pots and kettles in all shapes and sizes. Tristan eagerly watches how the witch mix spawn, mosquito legs, one leg owls, various powders, leaves, herbs, and liquid. After awhile, a stinky smell comes out from the pan. The thick green smoke fills the room which makes Tristan hardly breathe.

Tristan is a bit sick of the smell and he thinks that it's one of the witch's tricks to enchant him. But suddenly, the thick green smoke begins to dissolve and the smell disappears. A yellow smoke starts to whirl through the kitchen. Tristan takes a deep breath and smells a fragrant like a banana.

The witch grabs a spoon and scoop a bit of the potion to take a sip. As Drakonia puts the spoon in her mouth, Tristan pulls the spoon and pan from the witch.

Tristan looks at Drakonia sternly and says, "First, we are going to change the children back. If there are enough potions left, you can have it. Take me quickly where you keep them."

Drakonia comes up with small steps, tottering on her thin spider legs. She walks to the large wooden door and opens it with great effort. She picks up the lamp at the top of the stairs. She can't use any of her spells as she seems to have forgotten everything in her head.

Tristan runs after her and picks up the pan with the banana potion. He also takes the raspberry lemonade just to be sure.

Tristan looks at the lamp and a box of match on the table. "Go back to the kitchen and light the lamp," says Tristan to the witch. Drakonia nods and with wobbling steps, she walks back to the table. Moments later, she returns with a burning lamp. In the bright blue light, the witch looks frightening.

Drakonia can barely walk down the stairs on her thin spider legs and Tristan can't run fast while holding both potions in his hands. Step by step, they both descend the long stone stairs.

When they arrive at the end of the stairs, they stand behind the massive wooden door, much larger and heavier than the door at the top of the stairs.

"Open the door," says Tristan to the witch. But the witch can only open the door by a spell she cannot even remember anymore.

How will Tristan open the door and save the children?

Chapter 8

The spiders on the other side of the big heavy door run around anxiously. They still don't understand what's happening. First they were walking on a path of trees and bushes covered with delicious cookies. Then a lovely princess welcomed them in her house.

Her house has been old and ugly but the woman is beautiful and very nice. She's wearing the most beautiful dress that the children have ever seen. Her smile is so sweet and fresh.

"Come darlings, come on. I'm sure you are all thirsty and I have delicious raspberry lemonade for you," as she speaks to the children.

She points to the inviting glass of lemonade on the large table. Indeed, the children are thirsty. Then one by one, the children grab the glasses and drink quickly.

For a moment, nothing happens and then suddenly, the children feel very strange and giddy. Then there are popping sounds everywhere, popping sounds of children turning into spiders.

The woman drives them towards the door from the kitchen to the long stone stairs and through a door of a dark, cold cave.

When they are all in the dark cave, the woman turns to them and mumbles an unintelligible incantation and shuts the big door.

The spider with the crown calls to the other spiders and introduces herself as Princess Esmeralda. She assures the children that everyone is looking for her and eventually they will be found soon.

But the spiders are frightened too much that the children can't hear her. They continue to bang around in the dark, bumping into each other and falling over.

Chapter 9

Meanwhile, panic erupts in the village. No child has come home from school that day and the parents are very worried. There is no trace of the children at all.

Most parents are on the street, looking for their children. They call out the names of their children and ask other parents if they know something...but nobody knows what's going on.

Fenne is one of the children who hasn't come home that day. Fenne's father is very worried and has yet to find her. Soon he sees a lot of parents on street who are all looking for their children.

Fenne's father decides to go the school and see if the children might still be there. When he arrives at the school, the father finds a dark and empty place. There is no trace of his child and the other children at all.

Just as he decides to turn around, he notices an old path. The candies and the delicious fragrance are now gone. The trees and shrubs are almost grown back on the path.

The father takes a good look again. He has lived in the village all his life but he doesn't remember the path that he sees.

He decides to follow the path. The further he gets on the path, the more bushes block his path. It seems like the bushes keep the father from the cottage.
After a difficult hike, Fenne's father suddenly stands outside the old shack of the witch. He looks through the dirty window, the house seems deserted. He knocks on the door but no one answered. He knocks louder once more and the door slowly opens.

The father steps inside and shouts, "Hey, hello? Is someone there?" He slowly walks through the kitchen to the half open door.

"Hello," he shouts.

Chapter 10

Tristan hears a faint sound high above him, a sound of someone calling out. Tristan calls out loudly, "Hello???? Down here! We are down here, help!"

Fenne's father hears a child calling out to him. He walks to the door but it was too dark to go inside. He looks around the kitchen and finds a candle on the table. He quickly lights the candle and walks back to the door.

As he walks down the stairs, he shouts "I am Fenne's father! I'm coming!"

When he arrives at the bottom of the stairs, he sees Tristan standing with a cauldron and pan in his hands. Next to Tristan is a woman with two very thin legs. The woman turns around and pulls Fenne's father. He cries in terror and the candle almost falls out of his hands.

Fenne's father thinks he's dreaming. He looks closely at the woman who has no face but a spider's web with bulging eyes and with legs like a spider's.

"What's going on here," he asks Tristan.

Tristan tells him about the children who have been changed by the witch into spiders by letting them drink raspberry lemonade. He also tells about how the witch got her thin legs and face covered with spider's web. Tristan also tells the father that he forced the witch to make a potion to turn back the children but they can't open the door.

Fenne's father listens to the story and looks again at the witch. If he was not seeing the face of the witch and her thin legs with his own eyes, he wouldn't believe the story.

"Is that true?" roars the father to the witch.

Drakonia steps back with fear and her bulging eyes get bigger.

"Zzzjaaaa," she says, terrified.

The father walks to the door and tries to open it but it is too big and heavy. No matter how much he tries, the door doesn't move.

He asks Tristan, "Boy, are you sure my Fenne is inside?"

Tristan nods.

The father pushes the heavy door with effort and the door slides a little bit open.

Fenne's father continues to push the door until the door opens slowly with grinding sound.

When the door opens, they see dozens of spiders walking back and forth through the cave. Tristan runs gently inside and says, "I have a magic potion to turn you back." But the spiders walk away from Tristan as if they are afraid of him.

Tristan pours a small amount of banana potion on the floor.

"Go on, please drink. Trust me," says Tristan in distraught.

The father of Fenne takes a step forward and says,

"Fenne, my little girl, if you drink that potion you will transform back to human. Please trust Tristan and convince the others."

The spider with the crown standing in the corner quickly drinks the potion. A little spider comes from the other corner ramping and together they drink the banana potion.

Nothing happens. Maybe this is one of Drakonia's tricks and the potion doesn't work.

Then suddenly, the spider with the crown on her head starts to spin and run in circles. What's happening? Another spider starts to move weirdly.

PLOP!! PLOOOPPP! PLOPP!!

Princess Esmeralda and Fenne look around in amazement. Fenne runs to her father and hugs him around the neck. They kiss and hug each other as they cry for joy.

The spiders are now eager to take a drink of the potion. Quickly, Tristan throws a little more on the floor and the spiders reach to the floor to drink.

Moments later, the sound of 'PLOP!' is the only thing they can hear.

After all the spiders have turned back into humans, Tristan realizes there's only a small amount of potion left. Tristan looks at the two potions in his hands and makes a decision.

He turns to Drakonia and says, "You deserve to be turned into a spider. Now promise me that you will never enchant a child again."

Fearful, Drakonia nods with her spider web covered face. Tristan waits until she gets to the back of the cave and says, "We're going upstairs while you stay here. When we are all upstairs, you may come up and find the banana potion at the top of the stairs."

Fenne's father leads the children to the stairs with Fenne still sitting on his shoulders. The children follow while Princess Esmeralda waits beside Tristan.

When the last child climbs the stairs, Tristan puts the cauldron of raspberry lemonade on the floor. Together, Princess Esmeralda and Tristan walk upstairs.

When they all arrive in the kitchen, Tristan puts the cauldron of banana potion at the top of the stairs as he promised.

Then they all walk out of the witch's old shack.

Chapter 11

The sun outside is shining bright and everyone looks happy. They have finally escaped the witch.

Fenne's father tells them to stick together and bring Princess Esmeralda home first and then walk to the village where their parents are.

Tristan turns to the old house and asks Fenne's father to give him a moment. He remembers something he must do. Tristan goes back inside and finds his backpack full of goodies in the kitchen. He isn't interested with the candies anymore so he pulls all the candies out. Tristan takes the big old book of spells into his backpack and walks out of the house.

The parents of the children are also on the way to the palace to tell the king and queen about their missing children.

Meanwhile, in the castle, the queen is staring blankly outside the window as big tears roll down her cheeks. The day is almost over and another day has passed without Princess Esmeralda.

But as the queen stares to the window, it seems as if she sees something in the distance. There seems to be two groups of people parading towards the palace.

As they approach, the queen sees that one group consists of mothers and fathers from the village. On the other group, there's a man with a girl on his shoulders and there's a boy and a girl holding hands beside him. Behind them are children skipping and laughing.

The queen doesn't understand what she's seeing so she takes a look again.

But wait, she sees a girl...a girl wearing a crown.

"Esmeralda," whispers the queen.

Suddenly, a ray of sunshine lights the crown of the princess and the queen knows for sure that Esmeralda has come home.

The queen begins to cry to the king and tells everyone that Princess Esmeralda is coming. The king hurriedly runs to the queen and stands beside her. They both run as fast as they can outside the palace. Along the way, they both announce that the princess is back. Charlie, the dog, runs around and barks with joy.

The parents have also seen the children. They start calling out the names of their children as they run towards each other.

Many mothers cry for joy, followed by lots of hugs and kisses.

Tristan, Princess Esmeralda, and Fenne with her father walk through the palace. When they come to the king and queen, the princess jumps to his father to hug and kiss him. Her mother puts her arms around them and cries for joy and relief.

The king put Princess Esmeralda back on the ground but is still holding her tightly. Charlie jumps to the princess as he wags and squeaks for joy. When the princess bends to hug her dog, Charlie licks her all over her face.

The children wave goodbye cheerfully as they go home with their parents.

Tristan looks around but his mother is not there. He thinks she is probably at home with his little brother and sister.

When everyone is gone, the only ones remaining are Tristan, Fenne, and her father.

The king looks at Fenne's father and asks him what happened and where he found the princess.

Fenne's father tells the king that Tristan found the princess.

"Tristan and Princess Esmeralda can tell the story better," he says.

The queen looks at Tristan and asks where his parents are. Tristan says that his mother must be very worried at their home with his little brother and sister.

The king commands their servants to quickly come and get Tristan's mother and siblings, as well as Fenne's mother to the palace. Meanwhile, inside the palace, the queen asks for tea, lemonade, and something to eat for everyone.

Tristan and Princess Esmeralda are seating next to each other on a large sofa while Charlie sits at the feet of Esmeralda.

Then the door opens and Tristan's little brother runs to him and gives him a big hug. Tristan's mother is carrying Benthe on her arms. Fenne's mother runs to her daughter and they hug and kiss each other.

While everyone sits quietly drinking and eating, Tristan and Princess Esmeralda begin to tell what exactly happened.

Princess Esmeralda says she was in the garden playing with Charlie when a woman appeared out of nowhere. She was so beautiful that Princess Esmeralda thought she was a princess too. That's the reason why she wasn't afraid of the woman and took the lemonade and drank it.

"After drinking the lemonade, I was a little dizzy and suddenly, I changed into a spider," she says.

"The woman grabbed me and put me in a box. She was mumbling and then suddenly we were in my room and she took a dress from my closet. She murmured something again and suddenly we were in an old cottage in the woods. In the dark basement, she put me out of the box and trapped me in a spider's web. There were three other spiders, real spiders, which the witch asked to guard me," tells Princess Esmeralda.

Then Tristan continues with the story.

The king is so mad that he shouts, "That wicked witch should be in jail! Go get her and lock her up! Lock her in the darkest prison!"

Tristan grabs his backpack and takes the book out. He gives it to the king and says, "This is the witch's big spell book. Without this book, Drakonia can't do any harm."

He gives the book to the king so he can keep it safe.

The queen goes to Tristan, grabs him by the shoulders, and kisses him on both cheeks. She looks at him earnestly and says, "Tristan, I'm very proud of you because you've been so brave and clever. You've saved my princess and all the other children."

Tristan looks at his mother who is very proud of her son and gives him a wink.

Princess Esmeralda gets up and whispers something in her father's ears.

The king laughs and nods. "Very good, a very good idea Esmeralda. Ask them yourself," says the king.

Princess Esmeralda runs to Tristan, grabs his hand again and says, "Tristan, do you want to live in the palace with your mother and siblings? I've always wanted little brothers and a little sister! That would really be nice!"

Tristan's mother looks very shy and doesn't know what to say. "Bbbuuut Madddam, wouldn't it be too mmmmuch to live in the pppalace," she stutters.

The queen laughs and tells her that the palace is large enough for them. She also tells her that it would be nice to have someone to accompany her as she's often alone in their palace.

Then the king says, "I propose to give Tristan a big party. It's a national holiday that we can call a Tristan Day. No one needs to go to school or work on Tristan Day. We shall commemorate Tristan Day every year for the bravery he showed to defeat the wicked witch."

Chapter 12

Drakonia the witch painfully climbs the long dark stairs and takes the cauldron with the last bit of raspberry lemonade. At the top of the stairs, Drakonia grabs the banana potion and slurps all of it, not a little drop left in the container.

For a moment, nothing happens and then...PLOP! PLOP! Drakonia is back to her human form again.

Well, not really...her beautiful face turns with fury as she thinks of the stupid boy who messed up her plan. She's determined to take revenge on Tristan and all the other children. She hates children more than ever now.

When she walks into her kitchen, she sees the empty spot on the table where her big spell book lays. Her book is gone!

Violently, she throws the cauldron with raspberry lemonade on the table as she shrieks around the kitchen. The cauldron with raspberry lemonade wobbles a bit, the potion sloshing over the edge of the container and spills on the floor.

Drakonia sees the cauldron wobble. She turns around, frightened, and steps into the spilled potion. The potion has made the floor slippery and her feet slips under her. Struggling with her arms, she pulls the cauldron and falls on the floor.

She feels the raspberry potion on her stomach, arms, legs, and when she opens her mouth to scream, the last trickle of the potion enters her mouth.

Furiously, she turns and looks around, screaming and screeching...

PLOP!!

A lonely spider crawls across the floor of the old house of Drakonia.

Since then, no one knows where Drakonia went.

CPSIA information can be obtained at www.ICGtesting.com
Printed in the USA
BVOW08s1950170816

459353BV00001B/35/P